The Funny Looking Frog

For Olivia, James, Vincent and Alexander

Published by Crazy Beetle Publishing
crazybeetlepublishing.co.uk

Text copyright © 2015 Louise Joyce
Illustrations copyright © 2015 Romana Staniaszek

ISBN: 978-0-9934929-0-7

www.thefunnylookingfrog.co.uk

The Funny Looking Frog

Louise Joyce

Illustrated by
Romana Staniaszek

This is a story about a funny looking frog called Harry. Harry lived all alone on a small island by the river Thames, close to the old bridge in Richmond, London.

One day a girl and boy sailed past Harry's island with their dog. "Look," said the boy, "it's one of those funny looking frogs we saw yesterday when we were at Kew Gardens. It must be lost. Let's take it back to its family!"

"What a good idea!" said the girl. "You don't get frogs like that around here. It MUST be lost!"
Quickly, the children searched the boat until they found an empty jam jar under the picnic rug to put Harry into.

Harry listened carefully to the children, excited to hear about the place where his family might live. He had only ever known life on his island, and it did get awfully lonely.

Suddenly, the sky turned very dark!
Before he had a chance to escape, he had been lifted high into the sky, in the beak of a huge angry bird.

"Yuk! You taste disgusting," said
the bird. "Are you trying to poison
me?"
"Certainly not!" shouted Harry,
as he felt himself falling faster and
faster through the sky.
He looked down at the
treetops far below and closed
his eyes.

Harry landed with a great big THUD!
He opened his eyes slowly. Luckily he was still in
one piece. A squirrel, sat on a nearby branch, was
watching him.

"Hello," said the squirrel, "who are you?"

"I'm Harry and I'm a frog," he said.

"Really? A frog you say! Well, I've never seen
a frog in a tree before. What ARE you doing
here?"

"Well, I was very nearly eaten by an enormous
bird and now I'm looking for my family. Have
you seen a frog that looks like me?"

"No," said the squirrel.
"I've never seen anything quite like you before! You don't belong in my tree."

The squirrel gave Harry a firm push. Once again he was falling through the sky, down, down, down to the grass below.

Harry landed upside down on something VERY spiky.

"Ouch!" he shrieked.

"PLEASE get off my back, you silly creature," it said.

The voice belonged to a rather grumpy looking hedgehog,

who was not amused to have his morning nap interrupted.

Harry rolled himself onto the ground and turned to look at the hedgehog.

"What a funny looking frog you are," said the hedgehog. "Do you make a habit of falling from the sky?"

"Definitely not!" said Harry. "It's a long story, but I'm looking for my family. Have you seen a frog that looks like me?"

"I've NEVER seen one like you. But you could try the lake. There are lots and lots of frogs there."

Harry hopped over to the lake and
looked around. Two very fat
green frogs landed with a splosh in
front of him. The frogs looked very
funny to Harry.

"Well, well, well, what do we have here?"
said the largest frog unkindly.
"Looks like you're going to a fancy dress
party. Whoever saw a yellow and black
frog? Haha!"

"What do you mean?" said Harry nervously.
"I'm not going to a party. I'm looking for my family.
I was told I might find them here. Have YOU seen a frog
that looks like me?"

"NOBODY has ever seen a frog like
you!" said the smaller one. "You don't
belong here. Go away!"

Harry turned around and hopped away from the lake. He was feeling very lonely and didn't seem to belong anywhere.

"Hey, cheer up, why the sad face?"

Harry looked around. Was that a voice he could hear?

"Hey, you, over here!"

There it was again. The voice was coming from the red bicycle.

"Me?" said Harry, "are you talking to me? Are you really a talking bicycle?"

"What's so strange about that?" said the bicycle. "I don't wish to be rude, but you don't get many yellow and black frogs around here either!"

Harry turned away. He was too tired to argue.

"I'm sorry, funny looking frog," said the bicycle. "Please don't be sad. I'm going on a picnic. If you would like to join me, hop into my basket."

Harry thought about it only for a moment. He had nowhere else to go, and so accepted the bicycle's invitation.

It was dark inside the basket. Harry saw a mouse tucking into a huge feast of apples and strawberry jam.

"Hello, funny frog!" said the mouse.

"You!" said Harry. "It was YOU! There is no talking bicycle!"

"Teehee. You really think that bicycles can talk?" said the mouse.

"How green are you?"

"Well, not very green as you've already noticed. Have you EVER seen a frog that looks like me?"

JAM

Before the mouse could answer, they both felt themselves falling backwards
into the bottom of the basket.
"Quick," said the mouse, "we need to run before we get caught.
But to answer your question, no, I've never seen a frog that looks like you.
Well, not here in Richmond Park. You could try
that other place, Kew Gardens, I think it's
called."
And with that, the mouse
was gone.

Harry quickly hopped away. What could he do now?
He didn't know where he was, and despite his best efforts, he
was no closer to finding his family. He longed to be back on his
little island by the river Thames.
Looking around, he spied a large pile of logs and made his way
over. Making himself comfortable, he soon fell into a long deep
sleep.

Harry must have been asleep for some time,
as the sun was now beginning to fall in the sky.
He woke with a start, as something pushed gently against
him. Opening his eyes and looking up, he jumped in
surprise. Two huge black eyes were staring straight at
him. They belonged to a strange creature, who had
branches for ears and steam coming from its nose!
"Oh! Who are YOU?" said Harry.

The strange creature ignored his question. "What a funny looking frog you are!" it said.

Harry decided to be brave. "Well, I may look funny to you, but my name is Harry and I'm looking for my family. Have you ever seen a frog that looks like me?"

"I have never EVER seen a frog that looks like you!" said the creature.

Harry turned away, desperate to escape.

Across the grass in front of him, he saw a large shiny red car. Perfect, he thought. Cars go everywhere. Perhaps THIS car will take me to my family.

Harry leapt up and landed in the back of the shiny red car. In front of him was a bouncing brown and white puppy, its tail wagging excitedly.

"Hello!" said the puppy. "I'm Alf, pleased to meet you. But haven't I seen you somewhere before? Aren't you that funny frog we saw earlier by the river?"

"Yes, I think I am," said Harry. "But it seems a very long time since morning, and you wouldn't believe the adventures that I've had. Mmm . . . perhaps YOU can help me?"

The puppy had no time to answer,
as the door slammed shut with a
bang and the car started moving.
Very soon, it stopped outside a
redbrick house.
"Follow me, " said Alf. "I have a
feeling, I just might be
able to help!"

Harry followed Alf through to the garden at the back of the house.
"Wait here," said Alf, "I know two children who will be very
excited to see you!"
At that moment, the boy and girl came running into the garden.
"Look, it's the frog we saw earlier today on the island at
Richmond," said the boy. "I wonder how he got into our garden?"

The children knew just where to take Harry.
Carefully they placed him into the jam jar.
"Do you think he's going to be happy living
in Kew Gardens?" said the boy.
"Surrounded by his family?" said the girl.
"Definitely!"

Harry peered out from the jar and saw a tall lady with twinkling brown eyes smiling down at him. The children were speaking to her and she appeared to be nodding her head in agreement. She invited the children to follow her, pointing to the glasshouse in the distance.

"Bye bye little frog," said the girl to Harry. "We will come and visit you often."

"Don't worry," said the boy, "you'll be happy here. We will NEVER forget you. You will always be our funny looking frog."

Harry looked around in wonder.
His heart was bursting with happiness.
He was home at last.
Home with his family.
The family of funny looking frogs.

Lightning Source UK Ltd.
Milton Keynes UK
UKIC03n1647270716
279390UK00009B/42